I Love You, Bunny *by Alina Surnaite*

Lincoln
Children's Books

It was bedtime for Suzy and Bunny.

"I love you, Suzy! I love you, Bunny!"
said Mommy with a kiss.

"I love you, Mommy!" said Suzy. "But please don't go!
What if a monster comes when I'm sleeping?"

"Don't worry, Suzy," said Mommy. "Bunny is a clever little
bunny. He'll chase the monsters away. Now close your eyes
and go to sleep."

And Suzy did.

As she dreamt, Bunny
kept a lookout right beside
her, though the night was
peaceful and quiet.

But at dawn,
while Suzy was still asleep,
something dark came in
through the window.

Softly,
slowly,
a big shadow
approached Suzy
and Bunny.

It crept up to the bed

and quietly disappeared.

Suzy yawned. "Is it morning yet, Bunny?"

But her friend was nowhere to be seen.

"Bunny?" cried Suzy.

"Where did you go?"

"You left me
in the dark . . . all alone!
Who will chase the
monsters away now?"

Gathering all of her courage,

Suzy jumped off the bed

to look for Bunny.

Suddenly, she heard a strange, scratchy sound behind her.

What could it be? Suzy turned around and saw . . .

"A MONSTER!"

"MOMMY!" cried Suzy,

as she ran from the room.

"What's the matter, Suzy?"
asked Mommy.
"Did you have a bad dream?"

"A monster
ate Bunny!"
sobbed Suzy.

But behind them, someone sneaked in,

carrying Bunny.

She laid Bunny carefully on the ground.

"Meeeow," she said.

"See, it's our cat Misty
with Bunny," said Mommy.

"There was no monster in your room, Suzy.
Things can look bigger and scarier in the dark,"
she explained, "but it's nothing
to be afraid of."

Suzy picked up Bunny.

Then she picked up Misty.

Mommy was right!
There was no monster at all.

"I love you, Misty,"
said Suzy.
"I love you, Bunny."

"It's time to get a bit more sleep now,"
said Mommy, closing the curtains.

Suzy was feeling tired as she curled
up in her bed with Bunny and Misty.

But she knew that
she was **safe**.

There were no monsters to scare her.

To all the little ones and their fearless toys – A.S.

Brimming with creative inspiration, how-to projects, and useful information to enrich your everyday life, Quarto Knows is a favourite destination for those pursuing their interests and passions. Visit our site and dig deeper with our books into your area of interest: Quarto Creates, Quarto Cooks, Quarto Homes, Quarto Lives, Quarto Drives, Quarto Explores, Quarto Gifts, or Quarto Kids.

First published in 2018 by Lincoln Children's Books,
an imprint of The Quarto Group.
400 First Avenue North, Suite 400, Minneapolis, MN 55401, USA.
T (612) 344-8100 F (612) 344-8692 www.QuartoKnows.com

A catalogue record for this book is available from the British Library.

ISBN 978-1-78603-118-1

The illustrations were drawn in charcoal and colored digitally
Set in Didot

Published by Rachel Williams • Designed by Mike Jolley and Karissa Santos • Edited by Katie Cotton • Production by Kate O'Riordan

Manufactured in Dongguan, China TL 102017

9 8 7 6 5 4 3 2 1